# SARAH AND PAUL
# GO BACK TO
# SCHOOL

# SARAH AND PAUL GO BACK TO SCHOOL

## Book 1: Discover about God and the Bible

### Derek Prime

# CHRISTIAN FOCUS

Sarah and Paul go back to School - Book 1
© copyright 1990 Derek Prime
Reprinted 1995 and New Edition 2006

ISBN: 978-1-84550-065-8

Published by
Christian Focus Publications Ltd, Geanies House, Fearn,
Tain, Ross-shire, IV20 1TW, Scotland, Great Britain

www.christianfocus.com
email:info@christianfocus.com

Cover design by Andrea Raschemann and
Danie van Straaten
Cover illustration by Andrew Tudor, Allied Artists.
Black and white illustrations by Fred Apps.

Printed and Bound in Denmark
by Nørhaven Paperback A/S

You can now buy online at
www.christianfocus.com

# Contents

# Contents

To Amy, Katie and Jenny

# 1. The Holiday Ends

Paul and Sarah were twins. They were eager to start school again. Although they often pretended they didn't enjoy it, in fact they liked it very much. They were both excited about moving up a class. They'd heard a lot about their new teacher, and everyone who had been in her class before liked her.

'Are you glad you're going back to school, Sarah?' asked Paul.

'I think so,' said Sarah. 'It will be fun to go up, won't it?'

'Yes,' answered Paul. 'Miss Simon said that Mrs Fox's class is a very good class to be in.'

'I know,' said Sarah. 'She's supposed to be great at story-telling and she can draw well. Her class draws plants and things, and the drawings are hung all round the walls.'

The weekend before they returned to school was an exciting one for Paul and Sarah,

because it was their birthday on the Saturday. They had a lovely birthday party and they were given lots of presents.

There were some wonderful games to share, books and gift vouchers to spend. Paul had a new football and Sarah a painting by numbers set. Both their teachers at church had given them new hardback Bibles.

## Sarah and Paul

After the party Mum said, 'Why don't you go and collect together all your presents? You could tidy your bedrooms as well.'

'Oh, no,' groaned Paul. 'We always have to tidy our rooms! It's so boring!'

'Oh, yes!' replied Mum. 'Now you just do as you're told! Once you've tidied up you can enjoy playing with some of your presents.'

'All right,' said Paul and Sarah, with more of a smile on their faces now.

Once they'd finished, Paul went out into the garden with his new football. He enjoyed kicking it up against the wall, and then seeing how hard he could kick it as it bounced back to him. Sarah started her painting by numbers kit and was surprised how quickly time went.

\* \* \*

On Sunday afternoon they were looking through the books they had received as birthday presents. Sarah had an exciting book about Mary Slessor, who worked in Africa as a missionary. Mary's life had been full of adventure and working for God. Paul had a book about a doctor and his hospital in the jungle.

Paul turned over the pages of his book and looked at the photographs and drawings. As he read about some of the pictures he was very surprised. The book showed how people in some parts of the world did not worship the same God as he did. The pictures showed people bowing down in front of their idols made of wood and stone, which they called 'gods'. They all looked rather strange and ugly to Paul.

'Don't these people worship strange gods!' exclaimed Paul. 'Imagine carving a god out of a block of wood, or chipping one out of a lump of stone! It must take a long time to make them. But how silly to worship something you've made yourself. It's as stupid as worshipping one of those models I've made.'

Paul rather enjoyed model-making. The hobby had all started when his father had bought him a model electric train and track for Christmas. He had enjoyed making the houses and shops and crossings so much that when he had finished them he went and bought some other plaster-cast models to make, like Julius Caesar and George Washington.

Julius Caesar had been rather a messy job and the colours had run when he painted him. But just as he was remembering making the plaster-cast model he thought of something else too.

'Is there any difference really between these idols in my book and my models? Are these pictures of idols real gods?' Paul asked his mother.

Sarah wanted to know too. 'Why do they worship idols, if they aren't real?'

Before Mum had a chance to answer either question, Paul added, 'I'm glad I don't worship strange things like that!'

14

'Yes, I'm glad too,' answered Mum quietly.

Paul suddenly remembered something else to ask his mother.

'Do you remember that missionary who came to church? He'd been with a tribe of Indians in Brazil. He was the first outsider to learn their language. He did it because he wanted to write down the Bible for them. He showed

us a photograph of a man who had been a witch doctor. When he became a Christian he threw away all his idols and burned all the charms he'd used in trying to make sick people better.'

'Yes, I remember that,' answered Mum. 'There's only one true God, no matter how many gods and idols people may worship. And the one true God is the Father of our Lord Jesus Christ. But, you see, we live in a country where most people have heard about the Lord Jesus. People can hear about Him in churches. We can read about Him, for we've the Bible in our own language. But there are lots of people in the world who've never heard about the one true God and His Son, the Lord Jesus. So some

of them worship strange gods. They don't know the way to heaven.'

Sarah felt sorry for all the people who had never heard about the Lord Jesus, so she asked, 'Can't you get to heaven without knowing about the Lord Jesus?'

Mum replied, 'The Bible tells us that it's only through the Lord Jesus that anyone can go to heaven. Can you remember a hymn we sing that says that?'

Sarah and Paul thought hard for a moment.

Paul guessed it first. 'It's that hymn "There is a green hill far away". One of the verses says,

"There was no other
    good enough
To pay the price of
    sin;
He only could unlock the gate
    Of heaven, and let us in."'

Sarah began to hum the tune immediately.

'The hymn's right,' explained Mum. 'Only the Lord Jesus could unlock the gate of heaven. Unlocking the gate of heaven is just another way of saying  letting us into heaven. He is the

17

way for us to come to God. Men, women, boys and girls sin so much that they don't deserve to go to heaven. Indeed they deserve to be shut out. But Jesus Christ is the only one who can let us into heaven if we trust in Him.'

'It must be horrible to be shut out of heaven,' said Paul. 'Last term when my class saw a DVD I was shut out of the hall as a punishment because I talked after Miss Simon told us to be quiet. I didn't like it at all.'

'It served you right,' Sarah told him. 'Three times Miss Simon told you to keep quiet!'

'No telling tales, Sarah,' interrupted Mum. 'Just remember, it will be far worse for someone to be shut out of heaven. It will mean being shut out forever. But Jesus took the punishment which disobedient men, women, boys and girls, ought to suffer, when He died on the *cross*.'

Sarah thought for a moment.

'The Muslim boy down the street doesn't

believe in Jesus as we do. His family came from Pakistan. And then there's that Jewish girl whose father is a tailor. They don't believe that Jesus is their Messiah.'

Sarah thought for a second or two before asking another question.

'Do they need to believe in the Lord Jesus too to go to heaven? God wouldn't want to shut them out of heaven, would He?'

'No, He doesn't want to do that,' answered Mum. 'That's the reason He sent the Lord

19

# Sarah and Paul

Jesus to be our Saviour. God wants us to put our trust in the Lord Jesus as our Saviour. When we do, He's able to forgive our sins and to make us His children.'

Sarah looked at her mother and thought for a moment.

'But how do you know that what you say is right? Couldn't their gods be true gods?'

'That's a big question to answer,' said Mum. 'But the Bible, which is God's Word, tells us that these things are so. You'll find the answer to nearly all your questions in the Bible.'

'I'm glad we were given new Bibles for our birthday,' said Sarah.

'My old one was falling to pieces,' added Paul.

Mum smiled. 'Well, look after them, and - more important still - read them! Now who would like a doughnut and a glass of milk?'

# Get Active!

Find out about Mary Slessor.

Where was she born?

What other Scottish city did she live in?

What did she work as before she became a missionary?

Name the area of Africa that she went to work in.

What modern day African country is that area in today?

Look in an encyclopaedia or on the web for more information about her.

* You may check your answers on pages 106-7

# Art Attack!

Mrs. Fox told her class to draw things like plants. Draw a plant or a flower that you can see in your home.

# 2. Back To School

When Paul and Sarah woke up on Monday morning, the first day of the new school year, they were quite excited about going back to school; but they felt a little nervous at the same time. They had that strange feeling in their tummies - like when they had to go to the dentist! Mum could see that they weren't too happy, but she didn't say anything.

As soon as they arrived in the playground they felt better. It wasn't long before the whistle blew and it was time for school to begin. As they went through the doors the school seemed especially clean, as if lots of people had been scrubbing the floors and polishing the furniture.

Paul and Sarah went into their new classroom, together with most of their friends, and met their new teacher.

They were given tables at opposite sides of the room. It was fun having new tables and their classroom had been decorated during the holiday. Everything was fresh and clean. And everyone seemed well behaved that first morning of school - there was scarcely a whisper.

Mrs Fox spent most of the morning making her new lists of names, and giving out books.

'I want you each to write your name neatly and carefully on your notebooks, please,' she told the class. 'Your best hand-writing, don't forget. Now, while I finish all the jobs I have to do, please write on the outside of one of your notebooks the name of the subject as well - "English". Then write me a story called "My Holiday". Tell me what you enjoyed most while school was closed.'

Although Paul and Sarah sat at different sides of the classroom, they both wrote about their birthday party.

Paul also wrote about all his presents, including the Bible from his teacher at church.

His best friend, Philip, looked over and read what Paul had written.

'Fancy writing about getting a Bible,' he laughed. 'I don't believe all that stuff you learn at church. My Dad says the Bible is out of date. He says that no one who knows anything about science believes the Bible.'

Paul was just about to reply when the bell rang loudly for the end of school.

## Sarah and Paul

Paul and Sarah rushed home as fast as they could. They did, however, stop a few minutes to watch bricklayers building some apartments near their home. It was so interesting. Bricks and iron girders were everywhere, yet every man on the site seemed to know just what to do, and where everything went.

When at last they did arrive home, they burst through the front door, full of excitement.

'Look, Mum!' Sarah shouted as she undid her schoolbag to get out some of her new school books. 'We're going to have to work much harder this year at school.'

'We had to write today about what we liked most in the holidays.'

'What did you write about?' asked Mum.

'About our birthday party,' answered Paul.

'I wrote about all the presents we had,' added Sarah, 'and how we both got Bibles from our teachers at church.'

'We've brought home our new history text-book to cover, Mum,' explained Paul. 'Do you think Dad would mind our using some of that special paper he used to cover the book you gave him for his birthday?'

'That's a good idea,' agreed Mum. 'He won't mind at all, and there's plenty of it. Why don't you cover your new Bibles at the same time?'

'I hadn't thought of that,' said Paul.

'A good idea,' added Sarah.

'I'm glad you've both been given a new Bible,' answered Mum. 'Did you know that when Queen Elizabeth was crowned, she was presented with a Bible? She was given it because the Bible's the most important book in the world.'

'Why is it?' Paul and Sarah almost asked together.

'That's a big question to answer when I'm getting dinner ready! But the answer is because it's God's Book. Although lots of different men - probably as many as forty - wrote it, God made them want to write and helped them so that all they wrote is true.'

Sarah, like Paul, was always full of questions. 'Did those men know they were writing down God's words which would eventually be put together in one big book?'

'We don't know the answer to that,' replied Mum. 'Probably most of them knew that God was making them speak and write something special.

I don't think though they would have guessed that their writings would be made one day into one book like the Bible. That makes it rather wonderful. God had a perfect plan from

30

the beginning for all they wrote, although they didn't know it.'

'Philip looked over my shoulder and when he saw I was writing about my birthday presents and my new Bible, he laughed at me,' Paul said.

'Why did he do that?' asked Mum.

'He said something about the Bible being out of date, and that no one who knows science believes it,' Paul replied. 'I knew he wasn't right. But I didn't have a chance to reply because the  bell rang for the end of school.'

Mum looked sad. 'I'm afraid lots of people think and talk like Philip. They are out of date, and not the Bible. Many scientists believe the Bible is true. Mr Jones, the science teacher at the high school you will attend later, is a well-qualified scientist. He believes the Bible is true and reads it every day. Do you know what archaeologists and geologists are?'

## Sarah and Paul

Sarah answered right away. 'I saw a film on television about archaeologists. They dig up things from the earth and tell you from the pots and other things they find how people lived thousands of years ago.'

'A geologist studies stones and rocks,' added Paul, 'and can tell you how old the earth is.'

'You've the right idea,' replied Mum. 'Lots of things archaeologists and geologists have found out show that the history and the order of creation given in the Bible are true. So don't think that science and the

Bible won't go together! But I believe the Bible is true for lots of other good reasons.'

'Tell us some of them, please,' urged Sarah.

'Oh dear,' said Mum, looking at the clock, 'just look at the time! Dad will soon be home and I haven't finished getting his tea ready.

You'd better finish covering your books, and after dinner you can ask Dad why he believes the Bible is true.'

'All right,' replied Paul and Sarah. 'We know where all the things are.'

# *Bible Search!*

1. Part of this book was written by a shepherd. It has lots of poems. (SLPASM)

2. The name of this book means beginning. What book is this? (EGSEINS)

3. This book is about David's great grandmother. (HUTR)

4. Paul wrote letters to churches and individuals. Two of these letters were written to a young man. What was his name? (ITOYTMH)

* You may check your answers on pages 106-7

# 3. The Best Book

Paul and Sarah had decided how they were going to cover their history books and Bibles. They had seen Dad cover his book a few weeks before. He had bought wrapping paper, printed to look like real leather. To strengthen the paper he had put strong brown paper underneath it. Then he had covered the wrapping paper with transparent plastic, which was sticky on one side. By turning the plastic over the edges of the paper, all three layers were firmly held together. Then he had fixed the new jacket to the top and bottom of the book with a strip of tape, inside the stiff covers.

The twins knew there had been quite a lot of wrapping paper left and that it had been put in the bottom of the kitchen cupboard with the brown paper. They were sure their Dad wouldn't mind them using it, especially as it was for covering their school books and their Bibles.

It was great fun copying what their father had done, although they made quite a mess. There were bits of paper everywhere - on the table and on the floor as well!

When Mum came in to ask Sarah to set the table for dinner she was horrified to see the mess.

'You two rascals!' she shouted. 'Look at all these pieces of paper! You're so untidy. Clear it up at once, or up to bed you go.'

# Sarah and Paul

'We'll do it right away,' Sarah promised.

Quickly the twins set about clearing up.

\* \* \*

'Look what we've been doing!' said Paul.

Paul and Sarah's Dad had hardly settled down in his armchair after dinner before they showed him the new Bibles and the history books with their smart covers.

Dad looked at the covers.

'Where did you get that wrapping paper?' he asked. 'I know what's happened. Someone has raided the cupboard in the kitchen. I'll take the price of that paper from your pocket money!' He said this, pretending to be cross, but he couldn't keep from smiling, especially when he saw how worried the twins looked.

## Sarah and Paul

'Mum said we could use it and you wouldn't mind,' explained Paul, not sure whether his father was teasing or not.

Sarah thought she would change the subject quickly. 'She said you would tell us why you are sure the Bible is true, Dad.'

'Did she indeed!' he said. 'Well, I'll do my best. I'm sure there are lots of reasons I can give you. Let's begin with the age of the Bible. The Bible is the oldest book we have and it goes back further than any history book.'

Paul interrupted, 'When we got our new history books at school today, Dad, Mrs Fox said we were very fortunate to have them. Some of the books last year's class used were quite old, and even a bit out of date. Our new books have just been printed. We have a marvellous geography book too with lots of maps and photographs.'

'Yes,' replied Dad. 'New books are always being written. Some of the science textbooks I had to read when I was at school would be no use to you because scientists know so much more now  that the old books are out of date. But the Bible's never out of date. It's studied and read as much as ever. More copies of the Bible are sold every day in the world than most other books?'

'I didn't know that,' said Paul.

'Don't forget too,' continued Dad, 'that it's amazing you have the Bible at all, at church or anywhere else. Often men have tried to destroy it. They've burned all the copies they could find, but they've never been able to get rid of it. Because the Bible is God's Book, He's kept it safe. In fact, there are more copies in the world now than ever before.'

## Sarah and Paul

Sarah said, 'I didn't know until Mum told us this afternoon that about forty men helped to write the Bible.'

'The amazing thing about that, Sarah, is that they all agree as much as they do. They didn't all write at the same time. The Bible took about a thousand years to write, and the writers didn't all speak the same language. They came from different countries. And yet the stories and writings fit together into one book. God had a plan for the Bible, just as an architect has a plan for a house, to help the builders put everything in its right place.'

'I hadn't thought of that,' said Sarah. 'We watched the builders across the street this afternoon. It seemed so confusing. I couldn't help wondering how they knew where to put everything.'

Dad smiled, knowing what she meant.

Paul suddenly thought of something he had heard his father say before. 'Dad!' he said,

44

'you believe, don't you, that the Bible is true as well because so many things it says would happen have happened?'

'You have a good memory,' answered Dad. 'No one would have thought when my granddad was a boy that the Jews would return to Palestine and be a nation called Israel; but the Bible, hundreds of years ago, said this would happen. You know, of course, that the Old Testament was written a long time before the New Testament. Some of God's messengers in the Old Testament - the

45

prophets as they were called - had a lot to say about the Lord Jesus even before He was born at Bethlehem.'

'What did they say?' asked Paul.

'They said where He would be born, what would happen during His life, and most important of all how He would die and come to life again.' Dad explained. 'Everything they said came exactly true. It was only because God told them these things that they knew what was going to happen. We don't know what is going to happen next year, quite apart from hundreds of years from now.'

Sarah remembered something. 'At church,' she said, 'we heard how missionaries spend time putting the Bible into other people's

46

languages so they can read it themselves.'

'There's a very important reason for that,' answered Dad, 'and it explains again why the Bible is true. The Bible changes people's lives more than any other book in the world. It can change the unhappy lives of the fiercest tribe of South American Indians, and it can make a bad boy or girl good.'

'How can it do that?' asked Paul. 'I'm always getting into trouble! Either I make a mess, or I leave my room untidy. I keep making promises to do better, but I can never keep them.'

'I think you know the answer to that question, Paul,' replied Mr MacDonald. 'The Bible can make our lives better because it tells us how to become God's children through believing that the Lord Jesus died for our sins on the cross. And if we believe this message, it can teach us how to please God in our lives.'

Paul looked thoughtful. 'I hope I'll be able to tell Philip some of these things.'

# Get Active!

Art Attack: During your next visit to a beach or forest find different kinds of stones. Take them home to your garden and lay them out as a rockery. Decorate some as paperweights.

# Bible Search!

1. How many books are in the Bible?

2. What does the word 'Bible' mean?

3. How many books are there in the Bible that have someone's name as the title?

4. The Old Testament has more books in it than the New. True or false?

5. Look up the following Bible verses. What do they tell you about God's word? Psalm 33:4; Psalm 119:105; Proverbs 30:5; Hebrews 4:12; Matthew 24:35.

6. What should we do with God's word? Read the following verses to find out. Psalm 119:11; Psalm 119:81; James 1:22.

* You may check your answers on pages 106-7

# 4. Philip's Questions

Paul and Sarah walked home from school the next day with Philip. Paul told Philip how they had covered their new Bibles as well as their text-books. He also told him some of the things his father had explained about the Bible.

'My Dad says that people who believe the Bible don't know what's happening around them,' jeered Philip.

'The Bible's a wonderful book,' replied Paul. 'It tells us the answer to lots of questions which can't be found anywhere else.'

'All right then,' said Philip, 'tell me the answer to some of my questions. If Adam and Eve were the first people in the world, what language did they speak?'

'I don't know the answer to that,' Sarah whispered to Paul.

'Nor do I,' admitted Paul taken aback.

Philip asked some more questions and Sarah and Paul couldn't answer these either.

'There you are,' said Philip, 'the Bible doesn't tell you the answers to any questions!'

At this Philip pulled Paul's schoolbag and threw it on the pavement.

Paul tried to get even by grabbing Philip's schoolbag.

Philip snatched at Paul's jacket and caught hold of Paul's right-hand pocket. When Paul tried to get away, he heard a dreadful tearing sound.

'Look what you've done, Philip! You've torn my jacket. I'll get into big trouble now.'

But Philip ran on ahead.

'Mum won't like it,' Sarah commented.

'You don't have to tell me that,' muttered Paul with a groan.

* * *

When the twins arrived home, Paul knew he had better tell his mother right away about the jacket. She would be bound to see it before long.

'Look what happened to my jacket on the way home,' he explained in a sorrowful voice. 'Philip did it. It was all his fault!'

'You must have done something to Philip to make him do this to you. Were you taking something of his?' Mum asked.

'No,' answered Paul.

'Well, you were really,' interrupted Sarah.

'But he took my schoolbag,' said Paul, sticking up for himself. 'Then I grabbed his schoolbag; that was how it all started.'

Mum was really quite cross now.

51

'Never fight in the street,' she said. 'I know it's fun having a tussle now and again, but it's silly doing so in the street. A car might come along and knock you down.'

Mum sighed and had another look at Paul's jacket. 'I'm not so cross about your torn pocket because I can repair that, but I don't want you ever fighting again or playing about in the street. Do you understand?'

Paul could see how serious and cross his mother was and he knew she was right. 'Yes,' said Paul.

'Why don't you both sit down for a moment and cool down? One of your favourite television programmes will be on soon.'

* * *

By the time the twins' father arrived home Paul had cooled down, and his mother was sewing the pocket back in place. Sarah and Paul promised not to play about in the street again. They both realised how dangerous it was. Paul and Sarah wanted to tell their Dad about Philip's questions.

'Dad, we told Philip why we believe the Bible is true,' said Sarah.

'Yes,' added Paul, 'and I think he was rather surprised that there are so many good reasons for believing the Bible, although he didn't say so.'

'And he asked us some very difficult questions we couldn't answer, Dad,' continued Sarah.

'What were they?' asked Dad.

'Well, first of all, he wanted to know what language Adam and Eve spoke,' replied Sarah.

Paul added, 'And then he asked how the Lord Jesus could have been with God when God made the world, when He hadn't even been born.'

Dad smiled. 'Philip did ask you difficult questions, didn't he? Why did he ask these questions?'

Paul replied, 'Because he said that if the Bible is really God's Book it will tell us the answers.'

'Let me ask you a question then,' said Dad. 'If you wanted to learn some history, would you go to your geography book?'

'Of course not,' Paul replied. 'We would get out our history books and read them.'

'But wouldn't your geography books have some history in them somewhere?'

'Oh, yes,' Paul answered, 'but you wouldn't expect a geography book to have much history in it. A history book is full of history. Anyone who went to a geography book to learn history might learn a little. But it would be silly to learn history like that!'

'Yes, of course,' said Dad, 'but you see this is the mistake Philip is making. He's asking you a question which the Bible isn't written to answer.'

Dad pointed to Paul's Bible on the coffee table and said, 'The Bible is written to show us the truth about God and to tell us how we can become His children. Of course, it tells how God made man. It tells us about how God made man perfect and able to speak. But the Bible isn't written to answer questions about what language they spoke.'

'But the Bible does tell us things we can't find anywhere else about the first men and women, doesn't it, Dad?' asked Sarah.

'Yes, it does,' continued Dad, 'but that's not its main purpose. Philip asked you about the language Adam and Eve spoke; the Bible does tell us something about this. It tells us

55

that the whole earth spoke one language. Some people think that the first language was Hebrew - the language in which the Old Testament was written - but we don't know the answer to that really.'

Paul had been thinking

about something as his father was speaking.

'The Bible will have a lot to say about Philip's question about the Lord Jesus, won't it?'

'Why do you say that?' Sarah asked.

'Well, the Bible is all about Jesus and was written to tell us the truth about God.'

'You're quite right,' said Dad. 'Because the Bible isn't a history book, it won't answer all our questions about man, but because it's

God's Book it will answer our questions about God. Now what was Philip's question?'

'How could Jesus have been with God when God made the world, when He hadn't even been born?' replied Paul.

'Do you know the answer to that, Sarah?' asked Dad.

Sarah thought for a moment, and then said, 'Philip doesn't understand that Jesus is God and always has been God.'

'Quite right,' said Dad. 'The Lord Jesus is God. He's the Son of God the Father. Because He's God He has no beginning and no end. That's hard for us to understand. There was a day when you were born and there has to be a day when you die.'

'Oh, Dad,' interrupted Sarah, 'at school today we heard about Florence Nightingale, the famous nurse. Mrs Fox wrote on the board "Florence Nightingale, born 1820, died 1910". She told us to write it in our books and to try to remember the dates. Then she asked who could tell her how long Florence Nightingale had lived.'

'Yes,' said Dad, 'what was true of Florence Nightingale will be true of all of us. There's a year when we're born and there will be a year when we die. But the Lord Jesus, being God, lives forever. He was with God the Father when the world was created and He was with Him before the world was created, too. If we were to be saved from our sins, someone who was a man, a perfect man, had to die for us in our place, taking the punishment for our sins. But there was no man good enough to do this. So

the Lord Jesus, the Son of God, became a man so that He could die for us.'

Paul thought he understood now and so he said, 'Then that means that when

Jesus was born in the stable at Bethlehem it wasn't the beginning of His life.'

'It certainly shows how much the Lord Jesus Christ loves us,' added Sarah. 'No wonder the Bible wants to tell us so much about Him. I wish you would tell us what God is like, Dad. How can He be three persons?'

'Hold on there. Those answers need plenty of time. It's too late tonight. Perhaps at the weekend we'll have more time to talk. That is if you go up to bed at once.'

# Get Active!

Art Attack: God has no beginning and no end. Can you express that by drawing something that has no beginning and no end?

Write it out: Sarah and Paul's Dad explained in two ways why the Bible was written. Find the sentence and write it down.

# 5. Saturday Morning

Saturday morning was always special in the MacDonald's home. There was no school and as Dad didn't have to go to work Dad and Mum were able to stay in bed a little longer.

Now the twins were in Mrs Fox's class, they were old enough to make their parents a cup of tea.

The twins were pleased about this. They were given careful instructions because Mum was afraid they might burn themselves. They would take turns doing it - one Saturday Paul would do it, and the next time would be Sarah's turn.

They enjoyed getting up before their parents. On a Saturday their comic came with the morning paper. The one who was not making the tea would be able to read it first.

'Who's going to make Mum and Dad's drink first?' asked Paul as they went downstairs to the kitchen.

'Look, there's a coin on the hall-table. Let's toss for it,' suggested Sarah. 'Heads - you; tails - me.'

'All right,' agreed Paul, as he tossed the coin. 'Tails! Your turn, Sarah.'

Paul opened the front door and brought in the newspaper with the comic folded inside.

 He sat down and began to read it, while Sarah looked after the drink. When it was ready, Sarah said, 'Well, I've made the tea. You can take it up.'

'Oh, no,' said Paul, his head in the comic. 'Whoever makes it takes it up as well.'

'Now look,' argued Sarah,' you take it. And then I can look at the comic too.'

They started to quarrel. Mum heard them and shouted down the stairs, 'Say, you two! What's going on?'

'It's Paul!' cried Sarah.

'No, it isn't, you old tell-tale,' shouted Paul.

'Stop that kind of talk at once,' said Mum. 'If you can't make a cup of tea without arguing, I'd better come down and make it myself.'

'All right,' said Paul, looking crossly at his sister. 'I'm coming.'

'Bring up the newspaper too, please,' Dad called down.

64

By breakfast time Paul and Sarah were good friends again. Saturday was not a day to be spoiled by arguments. Dad would be home all day and sometimes they went out in the afternoon in the car.

On Saturday mornings there was more time than usual to read the Bible as a family. After breakfast, before washing the dishes, they got

* * *

their Bibles and read a passage together. If Paul and Sarah didn't understand something, Dad and Mum would try to explain things to them.

This Saturday, they were reading John's Gospel, chapter four, when they came to verse twenty-four. Paul looked a bit puzzled when his Dad read out, 'God is spirit, and his worshippers must worship in spirit and in truth'.

When they came to the end of the passage Mum asked, 'Any questions?'

'Yes,' answered Paul. 'What does it mean when it says that God is spirit? What is God like? He must be very different from us, although I suppose we must be like Him in some ways.'

65

'Yes, you're right,' nodded Dad. 'When we think of a person, we think of what he looks like. God is a person, but He has no body. That explains why He can be everywhere at once. Always remember that God is spirit, but that doesn't keep Him from being a real person.'

'It's rather hard to think of a person without a body!' said Sarah.

Her father smiled and said, 'Yes, it is to us because we've never lived without a body. Perhaps the best picture of God as spirit is your soul - it's the part of you which thinks and feels. You can't see your soul: and you can't see God. You can't touch your soul; and you can't touch God.'

66

'It's strange not being able to see your soul,' interrupted Sarah.

'Yes, but even so,' continued Dad, 'you know it exists because it's the real you. Although we can't see God, we know He exists, and we know what he's like. If I said to you, Paul, "What's your friend Philip like?" I  don't imagine that you would just say, "He's four feet nine inches tall with brown hair", but you would want to say things like, "He's my friend, he always asks a lot of questions, and we have a fight sometimes!"'

Paul looked a little ashamed, and wondered if his father knew about his jacket. But then he knew his mother kept her promises.

Dad went on. 'In other words, more important than what Philip looks like, is the kind of person he is. That's what the Bible does. It doesn't tell me what God looks like.

67

But it does tell me the kind of things God does and says.'

'Tell us some of the things the Bible says about God, please,' asked Sarah.

'Let Mum start,' replied Dad.

Mum enjoyed helping the twins to understand. She thought for a moment and said, 'First of all, God is eternal: He has no beginning and no end. Everything - like the clothes we wear, for example - has a beginning and an end. God always has been and always will be.'

'Now you tell us something, Dad,' asked Paul.

'God is infinite,' Dad replied. 'I'll try to explain what we mean by that. We are what we call "finite". There are lots of things we can't understand or do. We have to study to learn; and there's a limit to what we can know. But God knows everything. We can do many wonderful things, but sometimes a thing is too big for us. Nothing is too big for God. There's no end to His power. God is always greater than we can understand: that is what we mean when we say that God is infinite.'

'Can you spell infinite, Paul?' asked Mum.

'I think so - i-n-f-i-n-i-t-e,' Paul spelled out slowly.

'Your turn to tell us something more,' Sarah said to her mother.

'Well,' Mum replied, 'something the Bible often tells us about God is that He's holy.

He's without any sin. God has never thought anything wrong, or said anything wrong, or done anything wrong. He's so pure that He can't even look at sin. When we see something unpleasant or wrong, we find it very easy to be inquisitive and want to look at it. God is so holy that He doesn't even want to look at it. He can never like things that are wrong.'

Before Paul and Sarah had time to ask any more questions, Dad clapped his hands and said, 'That's all for now - we must help Mum clear up. Then if you two youngsters help me clean the car, we'll go for a drive this afternoon and we can continue talking then.'

'May I wash the car, Dad?' asked Paul.

'No, I want to do that!' shouted Sarah. 'Paul washed it last time.'

Not many minutes passed before Paul and Sarah were having another squabble over who was going to do what.

'I'll work it out,' decided Dad. 'Sarah, you clean the windows. Paul, you do the bumpers, the lights and the wheels.'

'I'd rather not,' said Paul. 'I'd like to do the windows.'

'Listen here, young man,' said his father, 'you'll do that or nothing at all! I'll wash the body of the car and then there will be no more arguments.'

Sarah and Paul looked a bit ashamed. 'Perhaps Mum will vacuum inside for us,' continued Dad. 'You can help her with that too, Paul.'

Half an hour later, when their work was complete, they all looked forward to their afternoon drive.

# Get Active!

Art Attack: Find out why the Bible was written. The answer is in the chapter. Write it down. Decorate the page with fancy lettering.

Real Life: Find out about Florence Nightingale. Where was she born? What was the name of the war where Florence nursed the wounded? Who awarded her the Royal Red Cross in 1883?

# Bible Search!

What words are missing from these verses?

John 1:14 – The Word became flesh and made his dwelling among us. We have seen his glory, the glory of the One and Only, who came from the Father, full of grace and _ _ _ _ _.

1 Corinthians 13:6 – Love does not delight in evil but rejoices with the _ _ _ _ _ .

Pslam 33:4 – For the word of the LORD is right and _ _ _ _; he is faithful in all he does.

Revelation 15:3 – Great and marvelous are your deeds, Lord God Almighty. Just and _ _ _ _ are your ways, King of the ages.

* You may check your answers on pages 106-7

# 6. Out In The Country

'Where are we going this afternoon for our drive?' Sarah asked her father.

'You can choose, if you like,' replied Dad. 'We can go to the park, or we could go for a ride into the country or to a forest and follow a nature trail.'

'Let's go to a forest,' cried Paul with excitement, 'and find a trail in the woods there!'

So as soon as they had had an early lunch

they set off. It was fun going out in the car. If they were excited about getting somewhere their father always thought of games the twins could play as they went along. This made the time go more quickly.

They started off playing some of their own games first.

'Let's play "I spy",' suggested Sarah.

So for about ten minutes they played "I spy", but they soon got tired of it.

'Let's do something different,' suggested Dad. 'It's to do with the names of the places we may see on our journey, and it takes a long time. We have to find the names of places according to the letters of the alphabet.'

'Which ones?' interrupted Sarah, looking puzzled.

# Sarah and Paul

'From the beginning of the alphabet, silly!' exclaimed Paul. 'Girls don't always use their heads!'

'Now, now,' interrupted Dad. 'We look for the name of a place beginning with the letter A. Then we begin to look for one with the letter B, and so on. We'll see how far we can get.'

'It's going to be hard to find one with the letter Z,' Sarah said.

Dad smiled.

'We'll face that problem when we get to it,' he replied.

'It will take ages,' gasped Paul.

'That will make it all the more fun,' laughed Dad. 'Whenever we go out together in the car we can continue playing this game, even when we're playing others.'

'There's the name of a town beginning with C,' shouted Paul, looking at a road sign.

'That's no good.'

'There's also one beginning with G,' added Sarah.

'No good either,' replied their father.

It wasn't long before they reached the forest. They had already found the names of places beginning with A, B, C and D.

'Perhaps we'll see an E if we go a different route home,' suggested Mum, seeing the twins were a little disappointed. 'So remember to keep your eyes open.'

Paul and Sarah were thrilled at being in the country. In school they were learning a lot about nature, so they wanted to look at as many different plants, trees and leaves as they could.

Suddenly Sarah noticed something.

It was a sign on a path showing the way to a beauty spot at a place called Erie.

'Look!' she shouted. 'I've found one.'

'Found what?' asked Paul.

'A place beginning with the letter E,' said Sarah triumphantly.

After a while Paul and Sarah were feeling hungry.

Paul sat down on the grass with a sigh.

'What is there to eat, Mum?'

'Egg sandwiches, Marmite sandwiches, peanut-butter sandwiches, crisps and cake,' answered Mum.

'Oooh, stop!' cried Sarah. 'I feel so hungry.'

'Let's stop talking and begin eating,' suggested Paul.

'Which grace shall we pray?' asked Mum.

'"Praise God from whom all blessings flow" would be a good one out in the country, wouldn't it?' suggested Dad. 'Why don't we sing it together?'

When they had finished the sandwiches, Paul was ready to talk again.

'Look at the lovely lines on that leaf I found, Dad,' he said.

'It's wonderful to think that God made all the things we've seen and collected this afternoon, isn't it?' added Sarah.

'Yes,' agreed Dad, 'and He made them all perfect, like the veins on Paul's leaf.'

'Is there only one God?' Paul asked, thinking of a question he had asked his Dad the other day.

'Yes,' said Mum.

'Is Jesus God too?' Paul then asked.

Again his mother said, 'Yes'.

'Is the Holy Spirit God as well?' asked Paul.

Sarah understood now what Paul was thinking. 'How can there be only one God, then? Surely there are three Gods - the Father, Jesus and the Holy Spirit?' Sarah asked.

Dad smiled. 'No, there's only one. He's the God who made the world and who has given us the Bible. He makes Himself known to us in three different Persons we call the Trinity.'

'What does Trinity mean?' asked Sarah. She liked finding out about new words.

'"Trinity" comes from two words: tri - meaning three - and unity - meaning one. The Bible speaks of three Persons - the Father, the Son and the Holy Spirit - but tells us they are one.'

'I don't understand how three things can be one,' exclaimed Paul.

'Let me try and help you understand,' replied his mother. 'Pick a clover leaf. Now, how many parts are there to it?'

Paul ate the rest of his doughnut before he reached for a clover leaf.

'Three parts,' answered Paul.

'But how many leaves are there?' Mum asked.

'One,' answered Paul.

'Look,' said Paul's father, as he drew a triangle on the ground with a stick. 'How many sides has this triangle?'

'Three,' answered Paul and Sarah together.

'All right then, how many triangles do they make?' he asked.

'One, of course!' they answered.

'How many of us are there here?' asked Mum.

'Why, four,' said Sarah.

'How many families are here then?' asked her mother next.

'Only one,' Paul and Sarah replied.

'Perhaps now you can see,' explained Dad, 'that there are many different kinds of oneness. Although God makes Himself known to us as three Persons, He also tells us that He is one, and that there is only one God.'

81

'It isn't easy to understand, is it?' Paul said thoughtfully. 'I wouldn't find it easy to explain to someone like Philip.'

'No, you're right,' agreed Dad, 'but remember we're talking about God who is very great and our minds are much too small to understand everything about Him.'

Sarah had a question. 'Did the disciples understand it, do you think?' She knew the disciples were just ordinary people.

'I'm sure they didn't understand it completely, Sarah,' answered her father, 'but I know that they believed it. They were Jews and they knew there's only one God, who made

everything. But then they met the Lord Jesus and they lived with Him for three years. As they lived with Him they came to realise that He was not only a man, but that He was also

God. They were very surprised to discover this.'

'They must have been,' commented Paul. 'Imagine finding out that your friend was God!'

Dad nodded and continued.

'Before the Lord Jesus left the disciples He promised to send Someone just like Himself to live inside them - the Holy Spirit. The disciples saw the Lord Jesus return to heaven. Not long after, at Pentecost, the Holy Spirit came to live within the disciples to give them power to be the Lord Jesus' messengers. They knew the Holy Spirit was God. But they knew He wasn't the Father. And they knew He wasn't the Lord Jesus, for He had returned to heaven.

So although they couldn't fully understand it, they knew that God is a Trinity, three in one.'

Mum had thought of something else. 'When you get home this evening, you could read the story of the Lord Jesus' baptism in the Gospels,' she suggested.

'The Lord Jesus, the second Person of the Trinity, was being baptised. As He came out of the water, He saw the Holy Spirit, the third Person of the Trinity, coming down like a dove, to rest on Him. Can you remember what happened next?'

'I remember,' said Sarah. 'Didn't God then say something about Jesus?'

'Yes,' replied Mum, 'at the same time, God the Father, the first Person of the Trinity, spoke from heaven, saying, "You are my Son, whom I love; with you I am well pleased." The Bible doesn't explain how God can be three yet one; but it simply tells us that this is the truth.'

Dad looked at his watch. 'It's almost time we were on our way,' he said. 'Let's pack everything and put it in the car.'

When they had packed up, the twins had a quick look round for anything they had missed. They walked along the hedges but couldn't find any flowers or trees they hadn't seen already. However, there were pieces of paper left from other people's picnics.

'Pick up the pieces of paper, please,' said Dad.

'Do we have to?' asked Paul.

'Yes indeed,' replied his father. 'When you've put them in the litter basket, you look at what it says on the side.'

So they picked up all the paper they could

see and took it to the basket. Attached there was a metal sign, which read, "Please keep the forest tidy".

# Sarah and Paul

Not long after, they were on their way home in the car.

'The windows are dirty, Sarah,' said Paul.

'I would expect them to be, with your messy fingers on them all the time,' said Mum, defending Sarah who had worked hard on the car windows.

They sped along the highway back to their home.

'Look!' shouted Paul. 'There's a letter F!'

'That makes three points to you and two to me, then,' said Sarah, peering out of the window to see if she could see the name of a place beginning with the letter G.

# Get Active!

Art Attack: Draw an ideal friend. Draw balloons and write words inside to describe this friend.

# Bible Search!

Now think of the Lord Jesus. He can be our friend too. Describe what He is like. Look up the following Bible verses for some clues: Proverbs 17:17; Proverbs 18:24; John 15:13. Are you a friend of Jesus. Look at this verse and see. John 15:14.

* You may check your answers on pages 106-7

# 7. An Afternoon Walk

On Sunday mornings Paul and Sarah went to their young people's group at church at 9.30. That was why their Mum and Dad had their longer time in bed on Saturday morning instead of on Sunday. There were quite a few things to be done before the twins went to church if their mother was to get lunch ready quickly after they all came home. Mr and Mrs MacDonald always met Paul and Sarah after the meeting of the group outside the church so they could go into the church service at eleven o'clock.

## Sarah and Paul

This Sunday Paul and Sarah were taught about something they had heard about several times before. It was all about how God made the world. Sarah was especially glad because she remembered only the previous afternoon she had asked her Dad whether God had made absolutely everything. She told her group leader this. She also told her about the trip she and Paul had had into the country, and

how many different sorts of leaves they had collected to take to school on Monday.

* * *

It was a lovely day as Mr and Mrs MacDonald, Paul and Sarah walked home after church.

'Could we go out for a walk this afternoon?' Mum asked Dad.

'Would you like that?' he asked the twins.

'Oh, yes please, Dad,' said the twins in chorus.

When everything had been cleared away after lunch, Dad said, 'We'll jump into the car and we'll drive up to the park. We'll walk to the gardens at the top of the hill, and then back again the short way.'

The twins particularly liked these gardens. Besides all the lawns and flowerbeds, there were some beautiful ponds, a well and a sundial to see and examine.

'What was your lesson this morning?' Mum asked when they were walking through the park, after they had left the car.

'Oh, it was all about creation,' answered Sarah. 'We read how God made the world.'

'Good,' said Dad. 'How about playing "True or False"? I'll say something about what I expect you heard this morning and you tell me whether it's true or false.'

'That's a good idea,' said Paul. 'Can either of us answer?'

'Yes,' replied Dad. 'But take turns to give the answer first. Then if you think the other person is wrong, you can give the correct answer. All right?'

Paul and Sarah nodded.

'The world just happened - by accident,' stated Dad. 'True or false? You start, Sarah.'

'False, Dad,' she answered.

'Yes, that's right.'

Paul had a question.

'How can you be sure, Dad? Mr Eaton said some people say it just happened; but that the Bible proves them wrong. But how can we be sure?'

'Don't you remember what you did yesterday?' asked Dad, thinking of how Paul had looked so closely at the veins of the leaf he had picked. 'Look! Pick that dandelion in the grass.'

So Paul went and picked it.

'Just look at its stalk and its petals. How perfectly they're made! What a difference between that and some of the artificial flowers we have at home!'

'It's amazing, isn't it?' said Paul as he looked very closely.

'Now, if you picked up a wristwatch, Paul,' continued Dad, 'would you say that it just happened?'

'Course not,' answered Paul. 'I'd say someone had made it and someone else had bought it.'

'Well,' said Dad, 'remember the dandelion you picked was far more wonderful than any wristwatch you might find. A wristwatch can go wrong and has no real life in it. But the dandelion has life in it and although you've picked it, its roots will grow another one in due course. Such a thing couldn't just have happened.'

Paul was quite impressed by what his father said and saw the point.

The sun had attracted lots of people to the park. Many of them were taking their dogs for a walk.

It wasn't long before they came to the gardens at the top of the hill. There were even more people there. But the gardens were very large, so there was room for everyone without being too squashed. The flower beds looked beautiful. There were great splashes of colour made by the clumps of flowers.

'God made the flowers after the birds,' said Dad. 'True or false?'

'False,' declared Paul. 'He made the flowers before the birds.'

'You've a good memory,' commented his mother. 'I don't know that I would have remembered that. I would have had to look it up in the Bible, I think.'

'Your turn, Sarah,' said Dad. 'The part of the Bible which tells us most about creation is Genesis, chapter one.'

'True,' answered Sarah.

'Look at that pond,' shouted Paul.

## Sarah and Paul

The twins ran very quickly to it. Their parents caught up with them slowly. It was indeed a splendid pond, full of goldfish.

'Another question for you,' suggested Dad. 'God created the world in seven days.'

'False,' answered Paul.

'No, true,' shouted Sarah.

'No, you're wrong Sarah,' explained Dad. 'It was in six days that God made the world. He rested on the seventh day.'

'Oh, yes,' said Sarah with a frown.

'Look at those lovely rose beds,' exclaimed Mum. 'They're going to be wonderful when they flower. I wish we had pruned ours as carefully.'

Paul remembered something Philip had said once.

'Dad, what would you say to Philip if he said to you, "How can you prove that God made the world?" He says, "How can you be sure, when no one saw God do it?"'

Dad smiled. He knew it wasn't an easy question to answer, and his answer wouldn't be easy to understand.

'You can't prove it if you mean proving it like proving two and two make four,' he said. 'But you see there are lots of clues all around us that confirm that God made the world.'

'What kind of clues?' Paul asked.

'Well, think of that dandelion you picked in the grass.'

Paul nodded, 'Yes it was amazing!'

Dad agreed, 'Well, if you see a painting, you know there must have been an artist. If you see buildings like these tall buildings that we can see in the distance, you know that a builder made them. If you see the latest model of a car, you know that someone designed it. Just look at those flower beds over there. Do you see how the plants are in perfect rows? Do you think that just happened?'

'Of course not,' answered Sarah. 'One

of the gardeners must have laid it out very carefully.'

'In the same way,' explained Dad, 'wherever we look in the world we see clues. We can see that everything that exists has thought and care behind it.'

'That's really what I said to Philip,' Paul said. 'I said to him, "If God didn't make the world, who did?"'

Mum laughed. 'That wasn't a bad answer.'

'Yes,' agreed Dad, nodding his head, 'but most of all I'm sure that God made everything because of what the Bible says. We know lots of reasons why the Bible is true - we've talked about them, haven't we? The Bible tells us time and time again that God is the *Creator*. I know God created everything, not because I can prove it, but because I believe what God says.'

Sarah asked, 'Does the Bible tell us how God made the world? Sort of how He did it?'

'No, Sarah,' answered her father. 'The Bible doesn't tell us that. You must remember that the Bible doesn't set out to be a kind of encyclopaedia on every subject! It sets out to tell us the truth about God and about ourselves. One of the first things it teaches us is that God is our Maker and all the good things we enjoy come from Him.'

'It will soon be time for us to go home,' Mum reminded them. 'Where would you like to spend your last few minutes?'

'May we go and have a look at the sundial?' asked Paul. 'I haven't been up here before when the sun's been shining. I'd like to see how the sundial works.'

It was fun trying to work out the time from the sundial. By the way the shadow was cast by the sun, they could see without looking at Dad's watch that it was getting late.

# Get Active!

Art Attack: Paul was impressed by just one leaf. See if you can find a leaf and trace it. Colour it in and draw in the veins. If it is the right time of year and leaves are falling off the trees, it is fun to see how many different sorts of leaves you can find. How about designing your own leaf cards for friends and family and tell them what you have been learning about God and Jesus Christ.

# Bible Search!

Are the following statements true or false?

1. The world just happened, like an accident.
2. God made the flowers after the birds.
3. God made men and women last.
4. The Book of Exodus tells us most about creation.
5. When God had made everything, He could say that it was very good.

* You may check your answers on pages 106-7

# Art Attack!

Here is an art project for you to do. Write down all the days of creation and what was made on each day.

Find old magazines or newspapers and look for pictures of these things to cut out. Paste them onto the paper beside the correct day of creation.

Beside day six put a thumb or hand print.

Did you know that no one else in the whole world has exactly the same thumb print as you do?

On day seven draw different things that you do on this day that make it special for God.

# Answer Page: Sarah and Paul Go Back to School

## Mary Slessor Questions Page 22

Mary was born in Aberdeen and eventually went with her family to live in Dundee.

She worked in the mills from quite a young age. Dundee was famous for it's jute mills. Jute was used to make rope.

She left Scotland to work with the mission in an area of Africa called Calibar.

This is now part of modern-day Nigeria.

## Bible Search page 35

Psalms
Genesis
Ruth
Timothy

## Bible Search Page 48

There are 66 books in the bible.

The word 'Bible' comes from the Egyptian word for parchments, Byblos, and the Greek

# Go Back to School

word biblios means books or scrolls. We use it today to describe God's Word, the Bible, which is made up of different books and letters.

True - The Old Testament has more books in it than the New Testament.

Psalm 33:4 - God is faithful. We can trust God's word.

Psalm 119:105 - God's word guides us.

Proverbs 30:5 - God's word is always true and God will protect us.

Hebrews 4:12 - God's word is powerful and it can change us.

Matthew 24:35: God's word will last for ever.

Pslam 119:11 - We should remember God's word.

Psalm 119:81 - We should hope and trust in God's word.

James 1:22 - We should obey God's word and listen to it.

## Florence Nightingale Questions Page 72

Florence Nightingale was born in Italy in 1820 and was named after the city she was born in.

She went on to become very interested in social welfare and studied to become a nurse before leaving to The Crimea War.

Queen Victoria awarded her the Royal Red Cross in 1883.

## Bible Search page 89

A friend loves at all times, Proverbs 17:17

There is a friend that sticks closer than a brother, Proverbs 18:24

Greater love has no one than this that someone lays down his life for his friends, John 15:13

You are my friends if you do what I command you, John 15:14

## Bible Search Page 104
1. False
2. True
3. True
4. False
5. True

# The Sarah and Paul Series by Derek Prime

Each book in this series features the MacDonald Family.

In *Sarah & Paul Go Back to School*, they're always asking questions: 'What is there to eat?' 'Can we go for a walk?'

They also ask questions about God and the Bible 'How do we know it's all true?'

You can find out about all the things that Sarah and Paul discover as you read this book.

In *Sarah and Paul Have a Visitor*, 4-year old Robert comes to visit. They learn some lessons about the Lord Jesus Christ during this time.

In *Sarah and Paul Go to the Seaside*, they

make a note of all the exciting things they want to do. They're staying in a cottage where there are plenty of places to explore. On their adventures they discover about the Holy Spirit and the Church.

In *Sarah and Paul Make a Scrapbook*, the twins find out the importance of forgiveness through the Lord's Prayer.

In *Sarah and Paul Go to the Museum*, Sarah and Paul see a golden calf that reminds them of the Ten Commandments.

In *Sarah and Paul Go on Holiday Again*, as they explore at the seaside, go on trips and have special treats, they also discover what it means to become a Christian.

# Stories from Canterbury Place
## by Catherine Mackenzie

We all face difficult issues in life and can often feel very alone in facing them. Sometimes we don't know what to say. Here is a series of books that will help. They deal with difficult issues in a fictionalised way and have such good stories that they can be read at any time.

**The Big Green Tree at No. 11**
*Tammy and Jake learn about life and death.*
ISBN: 185792-7311

**The Dark Blue Bike at No. 17**
*Tammy and Jake learn about friendship and bullying.*
ISBN: 185792-732X

**The Deep Black Pond at No. 12**
*Tammy and Jake learn about health and sickness.*
ISBN: 185792-7338

**The Lonely Grey Dog at No. 6**
Tammy and Jake learn about love and loyalty.
184550-1039

## Children's Devotions
by Frances Ridley Havegal

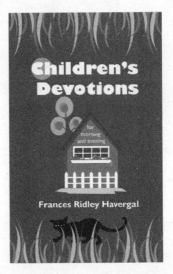

This was previously published as 'Little Pillows' and 'Morning Bells'. Frances Ridley Havergal, was a famous hymn writer, who also wrote gospel stories for children. Here are some of her best for thirty days worth of devotions.

ISBN: 185792-973X

## Jesus teaches us how to...

Sinclair Ferguson investigates God's word and the life of Jesus to find out the answers to fascinating questions. How are we to become wise? How should we pray? How do we be happy? How can we be kind? Find out all the answers, as taught by Jesus, in this imaginative and fun series that children will relate to and enjoy.

Jesus teaches us how to be wise   IBSN 1 85792 9829
Jesus teaches us how to be good  IBSN 1 85792 9837
Jesus teaches us how to  pray       IBSN 1 85792 9845
Jesus teaches us how to be happy IBSN 1 85792 9810

The following chapter is from another of the Sarah and Paul books by Derek Prime: *Sarah and Paul have a Visitor* where they learn all about the Lord Jesus Christ.

# Robert comes to stay

Very early on Sunday morning the telephone rang. Paul and Sarah MacDonald, who were twins, heard their father go down the stairs to answer it. They guessed by the way he was talking that there was some bad news.

'Yes,' they heard him say, 'we'll be glad for Robert to stay here. Why don't you let him come after church today? Then you can go off early tomorrow morning because you have a long journey ahead of you. ... Yes. That will be fine.'

Paul and Sarah weren't sure who their father was speaking to. They only knew one Robert and he was the four-year-old son of their parents' friends at church. As their father came up the stairs they couldn't hide their curiosity.

'Dad, we heard you talking about Robert. Was it Robert Tyson?'

'Yes,' answered Dad. 'Mr and Mrs Tyson have just received bad news. Mr Tyson's elderly mother died suddenly during the night. Mr Tyson feels that he and his wife must go south to where she lived as soon as possible. He needs to help his father do all the things that have to be done. The Tysons were wondering whether Robert could stay with us for a few days - it might be as long as a week. Of course, I said yes. Robert's coming to us after church. I hope he won't be too home-sick.'

'We'll do our best to help him feel at home,' promised Sarah. 'It will be fun having someone younger to play with. He can play with our toys when we're at school, can't he, Paul?'

'Yes,' nodded Paul. 'I'll get out some of my old toys that I played with when I was younger.'

'Have you remembered that it's Harvest Thanksgiving at church this morning?' Mum asked Dad. 'I took our gifts down to church yesterday afternoon. The children will take theirs with them this morning.'

'I'd forgotten that,' Dad said. 'I always find it interesting to see all the different gifts of food and flowers people bring. Have you children got your gifts ready to give to your teacher at church?'

'I've decided to take apples, oranges and grapes and I've tied a blue ribbon on the basket, Dad,' explained Sarah. 'Paul's taking tins - baked beans, of course, his favourites. He doesn't want a ribbon on his.'

\* \* \*

They could tell it was harvest-time as soon as they went through the church doors.

'What a lovely smell,' exclaimed Sarah.

'Doesn't it look good?' added Paul.

There were flowers and vegetables, fruit and

tins of all sorts of things. It looked like the inside of a supermarket!

'Look at that large loaf of bread in the middle, Paul. Isn't it huge?'

'Look at that pile of potatoes, too, Sarah.'

Mr and Mrs Tyson and Robert came and sat next to the MacDonalds and together they nearly filled the whole row. The children enjoyed singing the harvest hymns, especially their favourite one, "We plough the fields and scatter the good seed on the land." Robert couldn't read yet, but he knew the chorus, "All good gifts around us," and he joined in very loudly when the time came to sing it.

\* \* \*

During the afternoon Robert didn't seem unhappy about leaving his parents. He liked being with Paul and Sarah, as they played with him and read him stories.

After supper Mum explained to Robert about his bedtime. 'I think you must go up to bed now, Robert, as it's eight o'clock, and your mummy said that was your usual time.'

'Will the twins come to bed, too?' Robert asked, a hint of tears coming to his eyes.

'No, not just yet. They'll go a little later because they're older.'

'I don't want to go to bed on my own,' complained Robert, sounding very tearful.

'I'll tell you what,' said Sarah. 'Mum will read you a Bible story before you go to bed and Paul and I will come up with you and listen to it. How would that be?'

Robert nodded his head in approval.

'Get undressed first then, Robert, and as soon as you're washed and in your pyjamas, we'll have the story in your bedroom.'

The story Robert chose was the feeding of the five thousand with the little boy's lunch of loaves and fishes. When Mum had finished reading it she said, 'That was a good story to choose, Robert, on Harvest Sunday! Making the loaves and fishes go such a long way is what we call a miracle. It was easy for the Lord Jesus to do because He's God, and He made everything.'

'Yes,' added Sarah, 'in class this morning we were told that the Lord Jesus made all the food and flowers we could see in church.'

'Did Jesus make everything?' asked Robert.

'Yes, everything. All the wonderful gifts we see at harvest were made by the Lord Jesus Christ.'

Mum remembered Robert's singing in the

morning service. 'Let's sing "All Good Gifts,"
shall we?'

A big smile came on Robert's face as they
sang together -

'All good gifts around us
 Are sent from heaven above;
Then thank the Lord, O thank the Lord,
 For all His love.'

'I like singing,' Robert said. 'Can we sing
again?'

'Yes, of course. We'll sing again in a minute.'

Robert thought for a moment, and then said, 'What does Jesus look like?'

'I don't really know,' answered Mum.

'I do,' explained Robert. 'I've seen a picture of Him at church.'

'That's only a drawing, silly,' interrupted Paul.

'No, he isn't silly, Paul,' Mum corrected. 'Robert is quite right. Many artists have drawn pictures of the Lord Jesus and you can see them in storybooks. But you must remember that the artists are only guessing what Jesus looks like.'

'I'm sure He looks very kind,' added Sarah. 'The sort of person I'd like to have as a friend.'

'You're right, Sarah,' agreed her mother. 'The Bible doesn't give us a photograph of Jesus. Instead it does something much better - it tells us the kind of person the Lord Jesus is. It tells us He is perfect, loving and kind - the best Friend a boy or girl can have. Who's your best friend at school, Paul?'

Paul thought for a moment. 'I suppose Philip or Chris. Yes, I'd put Chris first.'

'Why is he your very best friend?'

'He's such a good friend. He shares things; he never lets you down; and he likes doing the same things I do.'

'It isn't because of what he looks like then that he's your best friend?'

'Of course not!' exclaimed Paul. 'That doesn't matter.'

'Then you can see why the Bible doesn't tell us what the Lord Jesus looks like,' continued Mum, 'but instead tells us the kind of person He is. He's the most wonderful Person who has ever lived on this earth. He was always kind. He never let anyone down. He willingly died to save His friends.'

'We'll see Jesus one day though, won't we? When He comes again? The Bible says so.'

'Yes, Sarah,' agreed her mother, 'and that will be a wonderful day.'

Mum looked at Robert and noticed how tired

he was looking. 'Into bed, sleepy-head!'

When Robert had climbed into bed, he looked a little unhappy. Sarah and Paul guessed that he was missing his own home and parents. Mrs MacDonald helped Robert to say his prayers. They asked the Lord Jesus to keep Robert safe until the morning and to bless his parents as they helped his grandad.

Mum was just about to switch off the light when Robert asked, 'If we close the curtains, Jesus can't see me, can He?'

She smiled. 'Yes, He can, Robert. The Lord Jesus is God and He sees and knows everything. Nothing happens anywhere without His knowing all about it. Because of this He's able to keep us safe. He sees me and He sees Paul and Sarah, and He sees your mummy and daddy too. And He watches over us all. He never wants us to be lonely. He always stays with us.'

'Even when we've been naughty and disobedient,' added Sarah.

'Yes and no, Sarah. The Lord Jesus doesn't leave us, but we don't please Him when we sin. If we're truly sorry He will forgive us, and help us to do better. The Lord Jesus is the best Friend you can have. He will always stay close to you.'

'I know a chorus about that,' Robert said.

'So do we,' Paul and Sarah chimed in together.

'All right,' suggested Mum, 'let's sing it before we say good night.'

'Jesus is with me all through the night,
Stays close beside me all through the night.
So I sleep safely till morning light.
Jesus is with me all through the night.'

'Good night, Robert. I'll buy you a Bible colouring book tomorrow morning. You can colour it while the twins are at school, and we'll talk about the pictures with the twins at bedtime.'

'Good night,' said the twins.

'Good night,' said a little voice under the covers and in no time Robert was asleep.

**CHRISTIAN FOCUS PUBLICATIONS**

Christian Focus | Christian Heritage | CF4K | Mentor

Christian Focus Publications publishes books for adults and children under its four main imprints: Christian Focus, Christian Heritage, CF4K and Mentor. Our books reflect that God's word is reliable and Jesus is the way to know him, and live for ever with him.

Our children's publication list includes a Sunday school curriculum that covers pre-school to early teens; puzzle and activity books. We also publish personal and family devotional titles, biographies and inspirational stories that children will love.

If you are looking for quality Bible teaching for children then we have an excellent range of Bible story and age specific theological books.

From pre-school to teenage fiction, we have it covered!

**Find us at our web page:**

**CF4·K**
*Because you're never too young to know Jesus*